Backyard Scientist®

A Science Wonderland
for the Very Young

by Jane Hoffman

Illustrated by Lanny Ostroff

Other Award-Winning Backyard Scientist books:

The Original Backyard Scientist provides children ages 4 to 12 a fun and fascinating introduction to science that makes chemistry and physics come alive. *Backyard Scientist, Series One* delivers more thrilling physics and chemistry investigations for the 4 to 12 year old student. *Backyard Scientist, Series Two* will astonish the 9 to 14 year old with thrilling experiments in chemistry and physics. *Backyard Scientist, Series Three* for 4 to 12 year olds shifts gears providing interesting investigations into biology, entomology, physiology and more. *Backyard Scientist, Series Four* is a great book to be enjoyed by the entire family. Nine to 14 year old students will especially like this collection of experiments that focus on chemistry and physics. *Backyard Scientist, Exploring Earthworms with Me* an American Booksellers Association PICK OF THE LIST is written for the 4 to 12 year old who wants to learn everything about these interesting and beneficial creatures with an exciting array of hands-on scientific investigations.

Backyard Scientist books are excellent for independent or classroom/group activity. They contain great ideas for science fair projects.

Backyard Scientist, A Science Wonderland for the Very Young.
Spring 2005
Library of Congress Control Number 2005900632

Published by Backyard Scientist/Jane Hoffman
P. O. Box 16966
Irvine, CA 92623
www.backyardscientist.com

ISBN 0-9618663-8-1

CAUTION! DO NOT EAT OR DRINK ANYTHING WHILE EXPERIMENTING UNLESS SPECIFICALLY INSTRUCTED TO DO SO IN THE EXPERIMENT. ALWAYS WEAR PROTECTIVE GOGGLES WHEN USING CHEMICALS. ADULT SUPERVISION IS REQUIRED WHEN CHILDREN ARE EXPERIMENTING.

Table of Contents

THE REVIEWS ARE IN ON THE BACKYARD SCIENTIST
WHAT EDUCATORS AND PARENTS ARE SAYING ABOUT THE BACKYARD SCIENTIST

"For the easiest and most enjoyable approach to science experiments, I recommend The Backyard Scientist by Jane Hoffman"

—Mary Pride
The Teaching Home

"Her goal is to see the public school system adopt an ongoing, daily, hands-on science curriculum. No one can say that Jane Hoffman isn't doing her part to try to achieve this aim."

—Nita Kurmins
Gilson
The Christian Science Monitor

("Hoffman's) own curiosity and energy are a large part of the appeal of The Backyard Scientist. I believe that science makes a difference in the way a child learns."

—The Chicago Tribune

"Anyone who can read, or get an assistant to read, can have fun building the experiments described in The Backyard Scientist series and then have even more fun using (Hoffman's) experiments to explore science."

- Paul Doherty.
Ph.D.
Physicist/Teacher

"What makes these experiments special is their hands-on nature. A firm believer that science makes a difference in the way a child learns, Hoffman encourages kids to think for themselves, to ask questions and to observe the world around them."

—Science Books and Films

"All of the experiments have been pre-tested extensively with groups of children."
—Curriculum Product News Magazine

"I believe that you have many of the answers to our problems with science education In the early grades."

—Mary Kohleman
National Science foundation
Washington, DC

"There are a lot of good reasons why you should order the books, but if you need another one, just remember you're doing it for a worthy cause—your students."

—Teaching K-8 Magazine

"Popcorn, ice cubes and string are among the materials used in her experiments...most of which the children conduct themselves. But the main Ingredient is the enthusiasm that Jane generates in the fledgling scientists."

—Women's Day Magazine

"...Backyard Scientist series is the best 'hands-on' experience a young reader can help him or herself to. Original and highly recommended for schools and home-teaching."

—Children's Bookwatch

"As a teacher, I truly appreciated your book. It was well organized and easy to follow. The experience with a variety of scientific concepts has sparked further interest in several areas with many of the students. They have asked for more!"

—Amy Korenack
Resource Teacher

"She makes science come alive."
—Orange Coast Dally Pilot

"Backyard Scientist teaches children the art of thinking."

—Anaheim Bulletin

"My mom is a teacher and thinks these books are the greatest."

—Ryan. Age 5

"I loved the Backyard Scientist Series. I like things I hadn't thought of doing by myself. "

—Chris. Age 7

"I loved the 'Backyard Scientist' books. They are so great. "

—Thomas, Age 8-1/2

"I tried your experiments with my students and they went wild with excitement."

—First Grade Teacher. Illinois

"I really appreciate the clear Instructions, simple to get household supplies, and the complete and easy to understand explanations. Thanks for these wonderful books."

—Mrs. Getz
Home Schooling Mom

Backyard Scientist, A Science Wonderland for the Very Young is dedicated to the wonderful home educating parents and teachers devoted to educating our young children in early childhood education centers, public or private schools and home schools. And not forgotten are the parents dedicated to supporting the formal educator.

Acknowledgements

A special thank you to all the home educating parents, public and private school teachers that I have had the privilege to meet over more than two decades and hopefully, in a small way assist you as you endeavored to educate our children.

It is heartwarming as I travel throughout the United States to see the dedication of the teachers that attend my in-services and all of you that came to see and hear me present at conferences. I know our children are in good hands.

Needless to say, I am grateful to the many tens of thousands that have used the *Backyard Scientist* books throughout the years and have provided such wonderful comments and suggestions, and who have encouraged me to continue my work.

There are many other special people that have encouraged and supported my efforts. You know who you are, and I thank each of you.

Family is important. I especially want to thank my parents, Sid and Grace for their support of my work as well as to my wonderful husband Arnold who encourages and assists me in so many ways.

I was inspired to begin Backyard Scientist by my son Jason's early interest in science. His inquisitiveness and thirst for knowledge of all kinds has never abetted. Now a successful young man and married to his loving wife, Amy.

To Victoria and Abigail, our youngest family members, may your lives be full of joy and knowledge.

I also fondly remember Millie, Leo, Lena, Joseph, Elliott, Evelyn, Jenny and Henry.

Welcome to the intriguing, mystifying and stimulating Backyard Scientist Laboratory. The laboratory features hands-on science experiments. Performing the experiments in this book will enhance your critical thinking skills and expose you to the fun and interesting world of scientific explorations. The experiments, while designed to be simple to perform, represent complex scientific principles to which we are exposed in our daily lives.

As soon as you begin experimenting, you will become a *Backyard Scientist* working in the real world of scientific investigation. Your laboratory is wherever you are experimenting, be it your backyard, kitchen or basement.

As a Backyard Scientist working in your laboratories, there are some very important guidelines you must follow:
1. **Always** work with an adult.
2. **Never** taste anything you are experimenting with except when instructed to do so in the experiment.
3. **Always** follow the Backyard Scientist directions in the experiment.
4. **Always** wash your hands with soap and warm water when you are finished experimenting.
5. **Be a patient scientist.** Some experiments take longer than others before results can be observed.
6. If you have any questions about any of the experiments, write to me, **Jane Hoffman, The Backyard Scientist, P.O. Box 16966, Irvine, CA 92623.**

HAPPY EXPERIMENTING.

Your Friend,

Jane Hoffman

Jane Hoffman
The Backyard Scientist

Experiment #1
Pin Cushion Experiment

Can you stick a skewer into a balloon and not make it pop?

Try the following Backyard Scientist experiment to discover the answer.

Gather the following supplies:
2 good quality latex balloons (9" works well), 1 wood cooking skewer and 1 tsp. cooking oil.

Start Experimenting.
Some teacher assistance will be required.
1. Inflate the balloon about a third of the way and tie the end so air does not escape. **Teacher may need to help tying the balloon.**

2

2. Slowly push the pointed tip of the skewer slowly through the thick end of balloon until it exits through the neck of the balloon.
3. Now dip the pointed end of the skewer into the cooking oil.
4. Slowly push the pointed tip slowly through the thick end of the second balloon until it exits through the neck of the balloon.

Can you answer the following questions from your observations?

1. What happened to the balloon when you pushed the skewer through it without first dipping it in the oil?
2. What happened to the balloon when you dipped the skewer into the oil and then pushed it through the balloon?
3. Did your balloon stay full of air or did some leak out, or did it pop?
4. What kept the air from rushing out of the balloon or kept the balloon from exploding in a pop?

Backyard Scientist solution to the experiment.

Most balloons are made from latex rubber. Latex molecules are members of the **polymer** family. Molecules that are polymers are long and skinny and can flow short distances like thick syrup. When you pushed the skewer through the wall of the balloon, some molecules were pushed aside and when the skewer went through the balloon, some of these latex molecules flowed and quickly filled the space between the balloon and the skewer. This kept the air inside the balloon from escaping.

The oil acted as a **lubricant** and made it easier to push the skewer into the balloon. We put a different kind of oil into the motors in cars to lubricate them so they operate the way they should.

NOTES.

....

....

....

....

....

....

Experiment #2
The Pea Puzzle

Where did the water go?

Try the following Backyard Scientist experiment to discover the answer.

Gather the following supplies:
A bag of dried peas, fresh pea pods, box of wood toothpicks, a large plastic jar with lid, magnifying lenses (students can share), strainer, measuring cup, small kitchen scale (optional) and a jug of water.

Start Experimenting.
1. Compare fresh and dried peas.
2. Spread the dried peas on a table.
3. Students should observe the peas for color, size, weight, shape, texture and hardness.

Teacher note. Record the observations on the board or on a large piece of paper.

4. Now begin the experiment which usually takes about two days to complete. They must be patient scientists.
5. Place the dried peas into the jar.
6. Completely fill the jar and record how much water it takes to fill the jar.
7. Cover the jar so water does not evaporate.

8. Leave the jar out where the students can observe it for two days.
9. After two days, remove the lid and pour off the remaining water through a strainer into a measuring cup. Record how much water remains.
10. Carefully spread the peas on a table and repeat steps 1 and 3.
11. Distribute some toothpicks to each student. The softened peas will become connectors. Let the students build whatever shapes their creative minds tell them to make.

Can you answer the following questions from your observations?

1. Before adding the water, describe the peas. Were they big or little? Were they hard or soft? Were they all the same size? How would you describe their shape? What color were they? Did they seem heavy or light?
2. Describe the peas after you removed them from the water-filled jar. Were the peas big or little? Were they bigger than before putting them into the water? Did their color change? What color are they now? Were the peas hard or soft? Did the peas seem to weigh more than they did before putting them into the water?
3. Were you able to pour out as much water from the jar as you put into the jar?
4. Where do you suppose the rest of the water went?

Backyard Scientist solution to the experiment.

The peas grew larger when they were soaked in water. The peas also became soft and mushy and could be easily squeezed. That is because the cells in the peas became filled with water molecules. The color should have changed too. Peas, like people, come in different sizes, shapes and color. The different size, color and shape do not make one pea better than the other and that goes for people too.

Teacher note. Spread the water-filled peas out on a piece of aluminum foil for a few days and let them dry. Let the students make their final observations using the same questions in "Can you answer..." 1 and 2. Also, save a few of the hard peas to tape to the chart.

Sample Chart

Name of Student	Observed Characteristics
Keilani	Hard like rocks
Jack	Small
Abigail	We poured in 2 cups of water

Experiment #3
Chemical Indicators

What can you learn from changing colors?

Try the following Backyard Scientist experiment to discover the answer.

Gather the following supplies:

1 head red cabbage, tap water, clean pot, strainer, coffee filter, a bottle with lid, eye dropper, clear plastic cups, safety goggles and things to test such as household ammonia, baking soda, washing soda, vinegar, lemon juice, crème of tarter, various antacid tablets, seltzer water and anything else you can think of.

Teacher note. Do this project over two days. On day one, prepare the indicator in front of the group and on day two have the students do the testing.

Start Experimenting.
1. Shred the red cabbage.
2. Heat water until it boils.
3. Add cabbage.

4. Cook until water is very red.
5. Strain through strainer to remove most solids.
6. Filter through coffee filter to remove fine solids.
7. Cool and pour into bottle and close lid. Store in refrigerator until ready to use.
8. Place different "chemicals" to be tested into clear plastic cups.
9. Using the eye dropper, place a few drops of cabbage juice indicator into each cup. **Solids that are being tested should be dissolved in distilled water as best as you can.**

Can you answer the following questions from your observations?

1. What color was the water before cooking the cabbage?
2. When the cabbage was finished cooking, what color was the water?
3. When you tested the different "chemicals" did they stay the same color or change when you added the indicator?
4. Did the color change to the color of the indicator or to another color?

Backyard Scientist solution to the experiment.

Scientists use chemical indicators to tell whether a chemical is an alkaline or an acid and how strong of an acid or alkaline. Another word for alkaline is base. Acidity and alkalinity are measured on a **P$_h$ Scale** from 1 to 14. Readings of 1 to 6 are acids, seven is neutral and 8 to 14 are alkaline or base. The lower the number, the stronger the acid and the higher the number, the stronger is the base.

The chemicals that were tested in this experiment did not change color. The cabbage juice indicator itself is what changed color when it came into contact with the tested chemicals.

You can make other chemical indicators by boiling rose petals or other flower petals and from tea. Test the same substances and see if you obtain the same colors. Different indicators turn different colors in the presence of the same substances.

Acids are sour tasting, produce a prickling or burning sensation when they come into contact with our skin. Some are in food or used in food preparation, but strong acids can be dangerous and poisonous.

An alkaline or base reacts with or neutralizes an acid. They usually feel slippery and taste bitter. **However, we should never taste anything when doing science experiments unless an adult says it is okay to do so.**

Experiment #4
The Dancing Popcorn Experiment

Can popcorn rise (go up) and sink (go down) in a liquid by itself?

Try the following Backyard Scientist experiment to discover the answer.

Gather the following supplies:
A dozen or so unpopped popcorn kernels, a bottle of chilled seltzer water or chilled carbonated water; a tall, narrow container—the taller and narrower, the better and a clock or watch.

Teacher note. Dry raisins work well too. They have a lot of nooks and crannies for the gas to fill.

Start Experimenting.
1. Place the popcorn kernels into the container.
2. Add the chilled seltzer or carbonated water.

Can you answer the following questions from your observations?
1. Did you see a lot of bubbles in the liquid?
2. What do you think they are? Make a guess.
3. Did the popcorn rise to the top of the water?
4. Then what happened?
5. Did some bubbles stick to the popcorn?
6. How long did the popcorn stay there?
7. Did the bubbles finally break?
8. What happened to the popcorn when the bubbles broke?
9. Did the popcorn then fall to the bottom of the container?

Backyard Scientist solution to the experiment.
The bubbles in the seltzer water are **carbon dioxide (CO_2) gas**. When you open the bottle, some of the gas rises up and leaves the water in the form of bubbles. Some of these bubbles attach themselves to the popcorn making them lighter or less dense than they were. These then float to the top and spin around and some stick together. When the bubbles break, the popcorn is then heavier or denser than the water and sink back to the bottom. This process will repeat as long as there is still a lot of gas in the liquid.

When your mom or dad puts floats on your arms before you go into the pool to keep you safe and above the water, they are changing the density of your body to keep you afloat.

NOTES.

....

....

....

....

....

Experiment #5
The Soda Straw Flute Experiment

Can you make sounds with a soda straw?

Try the following Backyard Scientist experiment to discover the answer.

Gather the following supplies:
3 plastic straws (not the kind designed to flex), scissors, tape recorder (optional), several small nails.

Teacher note. If you do this experiment carefully and you have a good ear, you can create your own soda straw band. If you have a tape recorder, record your soda straw band.

Advance Preparation. Before handing the straws to the students, pinch one end flat on each of two straws. Cut off the corners of the flattened straw to form two "reeds." This will result in a 'V' shape. Also, punch the holes in one straw. You will not have to do anything to the third straw.

Start Experimenting.
1. Tell your students that some science experiments take longer than others to "work" and also take a lot of patience and practice. This is one of those experiments.
2. Give one of the prepared straws to each student.
3. Students should insert the reed end of the straws into their mouths. They should not bite the straws or let their tongues touch the straws, but should keep the reeds flat by pressing on the straws with their lips.
4. Tell the students to blow hard into the straws. If no sound is generated, they should squeeze the straws tighter. If there is still a problem, inspect the reeds, they should be wide open.
5. Blow again. This takes a little practice.

6. As the students produce sounds, teacher(s) can go from student-to-student and clip off another inch from each straw.
7. Point out to the students the different sounds (pitch) they produce when the straws becomes shorter.
8. Pass out the straws with the holes.
9. Now have the students blow into the straws, covering various holes with their fingers.
10. Try slipping a second straw over the first straw (not the one with holes in it) to make a trombone. Slide the second straw back and forth over the first straw to change the pitch.

Can you answer the following questions from your observations?

1. What made the sound come out of the straw?
2. Were some of the sounds high and squeaky and others low?
3. What happened to the sound you made when the straw became shorter and shorter?
4. By covering different holes in your straw flute, did you hear different sounds come from it?
5. Was the pitch of the sound lower when the "trombone" was longer and the pitch higher when the "trombone" was shorter.
6. Did your class form a soda straw band?

Backyard Scientist solution to the experiment.

The sound that came from the straw was caused by air passing between the two **vibrating** tips. In instruments like the clarinet, flute, and oboe, these are called reeds.

The sounds you made in your first straw became higher the shorter your straw became. That was because it vibrated faster when it was short than when it was long. The shorter the straw, the faster it vibrated and the pitch of the sound we heard became higher.

Were you able to hear different pitched sounds come from your straw flute as you covered and uncovered different holes? Covering and uncovering the holes is like cutting off a piece of the first straw. Think about having to blow into straws of different lengths to make different sounds. Using a straw with holes is much easier. Using a slider to make the "trombone" was also easier than cutting off parts of the straw.

Sound travels in **waves** that are picked up by our ears and transmitted (sent) to our brain as electrical **impulses**. Our brains then **interpret** these impulses.

We heard that high squeaky sounds have a **high pitch** and low sounds have a **low pitch**. If you had an instrument called an oscilloscope, you could see the different sounds on a screen like a TV.

Experiment #6
The Roly-Poly Experiment

What is mass?

Try the following Backyard Scientist experiment to discover the answer.

Gather the following supplies:
1 potato as round or spherical as possible, knife, 1 plastic straw, a picture of a clown (have students color one as an art project), glue or plastic tape.

Teacher note. Cut potatoes in advance for students or let them watch as you cut them.

Start Experimenting.
1. Cut the potato in half.
2. Push the plastic straw into the center of the cut surface of the potato.

3. Paste or tape the clown picture to the straw (or cut two small slits in the picture and place on the straw).
4. Hold the straw parallel to the surface of the table.
5. Let go of it.
6. Do all of the above, but this time put the straw into the round part of the potato and with the flat part on the table surface.

Can you answer the following questions from your observations?

1. Did the clown bounce and move around in random patterns when the straw was in the flat part of the potato?
2. Did the clown bounce and move around when the straw was in the round part of the potato?
3. Why do you think the clown face moved around when the straw was in the flat part of the potato?

Backyard Scientist solution to the experiment.

The potato has **mass**, just like everything else. This mass combined with the round, unstable surface caused the potato and attached clown face to move when a **force** was applied to it. When the flat part of the potato touched the surface of the table, we had two stable surfaces touching and the same applied force could not move the potato and clown face. We could apply force in a different direction and make it move (slide the potato along the table). The potato will move in the direction in which we apply the force.

NOTES.

_____

_____

_____

_____

_____

Experiment #7
Surface Tension

Can you fill a cup higher than its lip with water without spilling the water?

Try the following Backyard Scientist experiment to discover the answer.

Gather the following supplies:
1 clear plastic cup, 1 paper or plastic plate, water, several metal paper clips, 1 eye dropper and paper towels.

Start Experimenting.
1. Place the plastic cup on the plate.
2. Fill the cup with water to its very brim.
3. Using the eye dropper, slowly add more water so that the level of the water is higher than the edge of the plastic cup.

4. In a moment we are going to add some paper clips to the water-filled cup, but before we do, let's predict how many paper clips we can add before spilling any water.

Teacher note. Record the students' predictions on a simple chart.

Student Name	Predicted No. Clips	Actual No. Clips
_____	_____	_____
_____	_____	_____

5. Now begin adding the paper clips while observing the surface of the water from the side of the cup.

Can you answer the following questions from your observations?

1. Were you able to fill the cup higher than its edge with water?
2. Why do you think you were able to over-fill the cup?
3. How many paper clips were you able to add to the cup before water poured out over the side of the cup?

Backyard Scientist solution to the experiment.

You were able, with relative ease, to fill the cup with water higher than the edge of the cup and to add several paper clips to the cup of water. This is possible because of a phenomenon called **surface tension**. Scientists also call this **molecular cohesion** which we talk about in other experiments in this book. This is caused by the attraction between molecules. All molecules have an **affinity** for one another. Some molecules, like water molecules, have a strong affinity for each other. Others, like mom's perfume or dad's cologne, have a weak affinity for each other. You can often tell which molecules have low molecular cohesion because you can often smell the molecules in the air.

NOTES.

_____

_____

_____

_____

Experiment #8
The Paper Tube Instrument Experiment

Can you make a musical instrument from a cardboard tube?

Try the following Backyard Scientist experiment to discover the answer.

Gather the following supplies:
1 core from a roll of paper towels, aluminum foil, plastic wrap, wax paper or similar source, 1 rubber band, 1 sharp pencil, and a 4" x 4" square of waxed paper or tissue wrapping paper.

Teacher note. Let students do as much assembly as they can. Teacher may want to punch the holes.

Start Experimenting.
1. Cover one end of the tube with the 4" x 4" paper.
2. Slip the rubber band over the tube and paper to hold the paper in place.
3. Use the sharp pencil to punch holes along the length of the tube.
4. Place the open end of the tube near your mouth and hum or sing into it.
5. Make some high sounds and some low sounds.

Can you answer the following questions from your observations?

1. To what orchestra instruments is this tube similar?
2. Did you hear sound coming from the end of your tube? Your classmate's tube?
3. How would you describe the sounds you heard?
4. Do you know how sounds are made?
5. Do you know how orchestra instruments make their sounds?

Backyard Scientist solution to the experiment.

You made a musical instrument similar to a **kazoo**. The paper covering the end of the tube **vibrated** when air and sound waves passed through it. If you sang into the tube, your friends could probably still tell that it was your voice, but it sounded different than the sound of your normal speaking voice. That was caused by some sound waves being **absorbed** by the paper and other sound waves being reflected by the tube.

Orchestra instruments make sound waves. Some are made when air is forced into the instrument causing it to vibrate—clarinets, flutes, oboes, trumpets and trombones, for example. Other instruments vibrate when you strike them—bells, drums and pianos. Yet other instruments vibrate and make sounds when something is rubbed on them—violins, cellos, etc.

Sound waves travel over distances. The waves act and look similar to the waves you make when dropping an object into a pan of water. They radiate outward from the source.

Teacher note. As an extension, you may want to show a video of an orchestra playing and together try to pick out the other instruments that musicians blow into to make sounds.

NOTES.

_____

_____

_____

_____

Experiment #9
The Truck Experiment

Does it take more force to start something moving than to keep it moving?

Try the following Backyard Scientist experiment to discover the answer.

Gather the following supplies (per student or group):

One or more toy pickup or dump trucks, a heavy-duty rubber band, plastic or paper collecting bag and small rocks of different sizes to fill the bed of each truck.

Teacher note. Do as individual, group or class project depending on number of available trucks.

Start Experimenting.

1. Have the class go on an "expedition" to gather a variety of different rocks and of varying sizes.
2. Categorize the rocks by size.
3. Attach the rubber band to the front or rear of the truck.
4. Half fill the truck beds with rocks.
5. Slowly pull on the rubber band until the truck begins to move. *Pay close attention to how far the rubber band stretches.*
6. Continue pulling it along at a slow, steady rate of speed. *Again pay close attention to how far the rubber band stretches.*
7. Now completely fill the truck beds with the rocks and repeat steps five and six.

Can you answer the following questions from your observations?

1. Before you tugged at the rubber band, was the truck at **rest** (still) or in **motion** (moving)?
2. Did the truck, when half full of rocks, begin to move as soon as you pulled on the rubber band?
3. How far did the rubber band stretch before the truck began to move?
4. Did the rubber band stretch farther when starting to pull the truck that was completely filled with rocks before it began to move?
5. How much farther did the rubber band stretch to get the truck full of rocks into motion?
6. Did the rubber band stretch more to get the trucks to begin to move than it did to keep the trucks moving at a steady speed?

Backyard Scientist solution to the experiment.

The rubber band stretched farther to get the truck started or to put it into **motion** from its **resting** state than it did to keep the truck moving at a steady rate of speed. Once moving, you only needed enough **energy** to overcome **air resistance** and **friction**.

Extra force was needed to get the truck moving in order to overcome **inertia**. The force, inertia, can be applied to something that is moving or standing still. We use brakes that produce friction to overcome the inertia of a car moving when we want to stop it.

Even more force was needed to get the truck filled with rocks to begin moving. That is because there was more mass and therefore there was more inertia to overcome.

Inertia tends to keep an object in the same state of **activity**, either still or moving.

When your mom or dad drive a car, it takes more gas to start the car moving than it does to keep the car moving at the speed limit. That is because your mom or dad need to overcome the force of inertia.

NOTES.

_____

_____

_____

Experiment #10
Building Paper Cup Towers

How tall will your tower grow?

Try the following Backyard Scientist experiment to discover the answer.

Teacher note. This is best done in groups of two or three students. Supplies are for a group.

Gather the following supplies:
A smooth surface to work on (counter or table), 1 pack of playing cards, a lot of two- to four-ounce paper cups (same size in each group).

Teacher note. Before you begin, form the students into groups of two- to four students each. This project will require some cooperation between groups of students and within groups. Each group will attempt to build a tower with the materials. Hint, the base should be built wider by using many cups per layer at the bottom and fewer cups per layer as the tower rises.

Start Experimenting.

1. Place a layer of cups on table.
2. Place a layer of playing cards on top of the cups.
3. Place a layer of cups on the playing cards.
4. Place a layer of playing cards on top of this layer of cups.
5. Repeat these steps until the tallest tower is standing.
6. When the towers are up, ask the students, *what do you think will happen if we quickly pull out one of the cards near the top of the tower without touching the cups?* **Teachers may want to try/practice this first.**
7. Have the students quickly pull one of the cards near the top of their towers.

Can you answer the following questions from your observations?

1. Were you able to pull any cards without the tower collapsing?
2. How many cards were you able to pull out?
3. How many cups stayed in place?
4. Do you think there is something on the cards that helped them slide out without disturbing the cups?

Backyard Scientist solution to the experiment.

It may take several tries to make the project work, but it is worth the effort and it is fun. Most cannot do this on the first or second try. A lot of different things contribute to the cups staying in place.

The cards have a smooth coating on them which makes it easy to slide them out quickly with only slightly disturbing the cups. When you slid out the cards, the cups did fall, but only a tiny bit—the thickness of the card—because of the **force of gravity**. However, as soon as the cup hit the cup below it, it stopped falling. Because there are more cups at the lower layers of the towers they were able to give support to the cups at the upper layers of the towers. They provided **structural support**.

Tall buildings are built using this same principle. Lower floors are built with more and stronger metal or wood beams than upper floors. Look for this the next time you go into an underground parking garage. Look at the size and spacing of the posts and ceiling beams.

When you are driving with your parents or on a field trip and you pass a tall building under construction, stop and look at the size of the beams and the spacing between them. Compare the size and spacing of the beams at the bottom to those higher up in the building.

Teacher note. You might ask an architect for some old construction or design magazines and go through them with the class to discuss how the buildings were constructed and see if the students can find the bigger and closer spaced beams.

Experiment #11
Using Energy from the Sun

Why do things get warm when they are in the sun?

Try the following Backyard Scientist experiment to discover the answer.

Gather the following supplies:
2 foam cups (any size), 2 thermometers, cold water to fill both cups, a digital stop watch or digital clock.

Start Experimenting.
Teacher assistance will be required.
1. Equally fill the two cups with the cold water (must be same temperature at the beginning).
2. Place one thermometer in each cup.
3. Place one cup in the sun and the second cup in a shady place.
4. Now check the temperature of the water and record the observations.

Sample Chart

Time (minutes)	Temp. Cup in Sun	Temp. Cup in Shade
10	_____	_____
20	_____	_____
30	_____	_____
40	_____	_____
50	_____	_____

Teacher note. When doing this experiment indoors, place one cup in a window and the other in a darker area of the room. Your results will be somewhat similar to the instructions in "Start Experimenting."

Can you answer the following questions from your observations?

1. Which cup of water became warmest?
2. Why?

Backyard Scientist solution to the experiment.

The sun gives off a lot of **energy.** Some of this energy is in the form of **light energy**. This light energy causes the temperature of the water in the cup placed in the sun to rise or get warmer. The temperature of the water in the cup you placed in the shade probably rose a little bit too, because it was heated by the surrounding air. It did not get as warm as the water in the sun as you can see from your chart.

If you did this experiment outdoors on a sunny but cold day, the cup of water placed in the shade may have become colder during the time it was outside. That was because no light energy could reach it and make it warm. It also cooled from the cold air surrounding the water. The cup of water in the sun may not have gotten very warm because the cold air was trying to cool the water at the same time as the light energy was trying to warm it.

Energy takes several forms. There is **light energy** that we just used in our experiment. Not all light energy that comes from the sun can be seen by the human eye. For example, there is ultra-violet (UV) light that we can't see, but if we go into the sun for too long a time, will result in us getting very harmful and painful sunburns. Moms and dads are always slathering on lots of sun-tan lotion on us to protect our skin from this harmful type of light energy.

Here are some other forms of energy. There is **heat energy** from burning things like wood in a fire place or a gas stove. Another form of energy is **electric energy**. We use electric energy to light lights and turn electric motors. Can you think of other uses for electric energy? There is another form of energy, **nuclear energy** made by splitting **atoms**.

Experiment #12
Fun with Capillary Action

Teacher note. This is a multi-day experiment.

Can you make water flow up instead of down?

Try the following Backyard Scientist experiment to discover the answer.

...then add a few drops of food coloring and fill the cup to the top with water...

Gather the following supplies:
2 stalks of fresh celery with leaves attached, 2 clear plastic cups, food coloring, measuring cup and enough water to fill the cups.

Start Experimenting.
Day One.
1. Show the students how firm and crisp the celery is. Let them touch and explore it.
2. Cut a piece off and squeeze it so water comes out.
3. Place one piece of celery into each empty cup.
4. Make several observations during the day.

Teacher note. Students may use describing words such as **limp, stiff, bends easy, does not bend easy, does/does not stand up straight, leaves droop or hang down, color is not bright,** etc.

Day two.
1. Observe the celery in the empty cups. Students should use their describing words from above.
2. Replace one piece of celery in each cup.

3. Measure how much water it takes to fill both cups.
4. Add a few drops of food coloring to one of the cups.
5. Make several observations during the day.

Day three.
1. Observe the celery sticks. Use the describing words to describe today's observations.
2. Remove the celery sticks from the cups.
3. Measure the amount of water remaining in each cup.

Can you answer the following questions from your observations?
1. When you started, was the fresh celery full of water?
2. How did the celery look at the end of day one?
3. How did the celery look at the beginning and end of day two?
4. When the water was added to one cup and water and food coloring were added to the other cup, how did the celery in each cup begin to look? What was different? What was the same?
5. At the end of day three, where did the water in the cups go?
6. Did it seem that a lot of water disappeared?
7. How much water disappeared or was absorbed by the celery?

Backyard Scientist solution to the experiment.
The **cells** in a stalk of celery are filled with water. You can see the water by cutting a piece of celery and squeezing it.

By leaving the celery stalk out in the air overnight, some of the water in the cells **evaporated** into the air. As the water evaporated, the celery became less stiff, the leaves drooped and the celery would bend easily.

When water was poured into the cup, the celery cells **absorbed** the water and the celery began to return to its original color and stiffness. In general, the celery began to appear the way fresh celery appears.

The water in the cup rose into the stalk to fill the cells that needed water. The level of water in the cup became lower as it was absorbed by the celery.

You saw the color of the celery change to the color of the food coloring as the colored water rose through the **capillaries** of the celery. Our bodies have capillaries too. They carry nutrients (food) to various parts of our bodies.

It is always best to store celery in the refrigerator in a container of water. The air inside most refrigerators is very dry and celery if left in it too long will become limp and will not taste as good as celery kept in water.

We all like the taste of crisp and crunchy celery and like the snapping or breaking noise when we eat the celery.

Experiment #13
The Strength of Air

Is air strong enough to hold up water?

Try the following Backyard Scientist experiment to discover the answer.

Gather the following supplies:
1 small plastic cup, 1 piece of paper board (like that at the back of a writing tablet or scratch pad) just a little larger than the opening of the cup, enough water to completely fill the cup.

Start Experimenting.
1. Fill the cup to the rim with water.
2. Cut the paper board so it is just a little larger than the opening of the cup.

3. Place the paper board over the cup.
4. Hold your hand over the paper board and turn the cup over so it is upside down. A little water may flow out.
5. Take your hand off the paper board and continue to hold the base of the cup.
6. Observe.

Can you answer the following questions from your observations?

1. Did the water pour out of the cup when you turned it upside down?
2. What do you think is holding the water in the cup and keeping it from pouring out?

Backyard Scientist solution to the experiment.

You did a magic trick. A lot of magic tricks are optical illusions based on real science principles.

The water did not pour out of the cup although we may have spilled a little turning it upside down.

The water was held in the cup even though we turned it upside down by the pressure of the air outside pushing up on it. Molecules of air pushing on the outside of the paper board were stronger than the molecules of water pushing down on the paper board from inside the cup.

NOTES.

_____

_____

_____

_____

_____

_____

_____

Experiment #14
The Gas Experiment

Can we use a dissolved gas to do work like inflate a balloon?

Try the following Backyard Scientist experiment to discover the answer.

Gather the following supplies:
One 12 ounce carbonated soft drink in plastic bottle, 1 balloon, large bowl, enough hot water to fill bowl, bottle opener, rubber gloves and access to refrigerator with a freezer section.

Start Experimenting.
Teacher assistance will be required.
1. Place the beverage bottle in the freezer over night. Try not to shake the bottle.
2. Remove it from the freezer when you are ready to do the balance of the experiment—do not shake the bottle.
3. Fill the bowl about ¾ full with hot water—hot from the tap will do.
4. Remove the cap and quickly place the balloon over the neck of the bottle.

5. Push the bottle down into the bowl of hot water—you may have to refill the bowl with hot water if it gets cold right away.
6. Hold the bottle at the neck so you are holding both the balloon and the bottle.
7. Now shake the bottle.
8. Observe.

Can you answer the following questions from your observations?

1. Did you see bubbles inside the bottle when the liquid was frozen solid?
2. Did you see the bubbles inside the bottle when the solid turned into a liquid in the hot water?
3. What do you suppose these bubbles are made of?
4. Did the balloon grow larger as the bottle was warmed by the hot water?

Backyard Scientist solution to the experiment.

You probably did not see any bubbles inside the bottle when the liquid was frozen into ice. Yes, there were bubbles inside the soda bottle when the ice melted into a liquid. The bubbles are made of **carbon dioxide gas**. Scientists use symbols for chemicals. The symbol for carbon dioxide gas is CO_2. This gas is **dissolved** in all carbonated sodas which are mostly made from water. The chemical symbol for water is H_2O. There are other things that are dissolved in sodas. Some of these are sugar or other things to make the soda sweet and flavors to make it taste good. Now you know you can dissolve gasses in water too.

In our experiment, some of the dissolved gas was released when the bottle was shaken. The colder a liquid is, the more dissolved gas it will hold. When we heated the bottle in the hot water, we raised the temperature of the soda and most of the dissolved gas was released from the liquid.

The released gas inflated the balloon we put on top of the bottle. There were more **molecules** of gas pushing out from inside the balloon, than there were on the outside of the balloon pushing in on the balloon. Sometimes, we call this **pressure**.

NOTES.

....

....

....

Experiment #15
Earthworms

Do earthworms make plants stronger and bigger?

Try the following Backyard Scientist experiment to discover the answer.

Gather the following supplies:
2 plants (identical kind and size), 2 eight inch pots, plain planting soil, water, four to six earthworms, 2 labels, a pen or pencil and access to a window or lighted area.

Teacher note. This experiment can take up to several months of periodic observations. Prepare a chart that you can mount on the wall to record student observations. You may want to build a wall made of aluminum foil around your plant(s) so that the earthworms don't "leave" the area. Also, don't over water the plants or the earthworms will not be able to respire. You may drown the earthworms if you over water.

Start Experimenting.

Teacher Assistance will be required.

1. Fill each pot with planting soil.
2. Dig a small hole in the center of each pot.
3. Place one plant in each hole. Be careful not to disturb the root ball when you transfer the plants from their original container.
4. Mark one label "Earthworms at Work" and label the other "No Earthworms in Here."
5. Press a few small scraps of apple or orange peel into the soil where your earthworms live.
6. Add the earthworms only to the pot marked "Earthworms at Work."
7. Place the two plants in a warm and well lighted area.
8. Water your plants regularly as needed. You may want to designate students to this each week and rotate the assignment to develop responsibility.
9. Occasionally add more apple scraps or orange peel to the soil and press into the soil.
10. Over time observe how tall each plant grows, the color of the plant, and its general health.

Can you answer the following questions from your observations?

1. Did one plant grow taller or longer than the other?
2. Were the leaves of one plant greener or brighter than those on the other?
3. Did one plant look healthier than the other?
4. Did both plants need the same amount of water?
5. Did the soil in one pot seem "looser" than the soil in the other pot?

Backyard Scientist solution to the experiment.

Usually, the plant in the pot containing the earthworms will look stronger and will be greener, brighter, and taller or longer. As the earthworms eat and digest their food (the apple scraps or orange peel), they leave behind **casings** that contain **nutrients** that the plants use to make them grow and be healthy.

Earthworms, as they **burrow** in the soil, leave tunnels which can hold water and allow air to circulate in the soil. Most plants like to be in damp, loose soil.

NOTES.

_____

_____

_____

Experiment #16
Buoyancy

Will it float or sink?

Try the following Backyard Scientist experiment to discover the answer.

Gather the following supplies:
One of the following deep and see through containers—gallon size or larger wide-mouth container, large fish bowl or an aquarium, water to fill the above, various objects—paper clips, small pebbles, different brands and sizes of soap bars, pencils, wood toothpicks, macaroni, rice, etc.—to test, and, two to three pounds of salt (amount depends on size of container) and a long wooden, plastic or metal spoon.

Start Experimenting.
1. Add water to the container until it is ¾ full.
2. Have the students predict if the object will sink or float before dropping it into the water.

3. Record the predictions.
4. Remove the objects after each student makes his/her drop.
5. Slowly pour salt into the water, stirring as you do until no more salt will dissolve in the water.
6. Again have the students predict if the objects they drop into the water will float or sink.
7. Repeat steps 2 through 4.

Can you answer the following questions from your observations?
1. Which objects floated in the plain water?
2. Which objects sank in the plain water?
3. Did the objects always sink all the way to the bottom?
4. Why did some objects float and some sink?
5. Did some objects that sank before the salt was added to the water then float after the salt was added to the water?
6. Did some objects sink all the way to the bottom in the salt water?

Backyard Scientist solution to the experiment.
Some of the objects dropped into the water sank while others floated. Some may have gone part way down into the water not reaching the bottom. Those that went only part way down reached what is called **neutral buoyancy**.

Were you able to correctly guess which objects sank and which floated in the water?

When the salt was added to the water, the salt dissolved and the salt **molecules** filled the spaces between the water molecules. Yes, there are spaces between molecules. Adding the salt to the water, made the water more **dense**.

Things that are more dense than water will sink. Things that are less dense than water will float.

Some of the objects that sank to the bottom in the plain water may have floated in the salt water or not have sunk as far down.

Water can be thought of as a lifting force. If the object weighs less than the amount of water it displaces, it will float. If the object weighs more than an equal amount of water, the object will sink.

The objects **displaced** some of the water. Displacement is the volume or weight of a volume of fluid (liquid or gas) by a floating body (like the objects you dropped in the water or by a ship) of equal weight.

Experiment #17
Building a Stethoscope

Can you hear your heart beating?

Try the following Backyard Scientist experiment to discover the answer.

Gather the following supplies:
A metal funnel, 4 feet of surgical rubber tubing to fit over the narrow end of the funnel (get at drug or building supply store), 1 two- to four-ounce paper cup, a sharp pencil, masking tape. **Teacher note.** You can use plastic tubing instead of rubber tubing.

Start Experimenting.
1. Teacher may ask, *for what do you think we are going to use the funnel?*
2. Write the answers on the board or large piece of paper.
3. Explain for what funnels are used—*to transfer things from one container to another container that has a smaller opening.*
4. Ask if they have seen funnels used before.
5. We are going to use the funnel for another purpose or use in this experiment. We are going to build our own stethoscope so we can hear our heart beats and the heart beats of our friends.
Teacher assistance will be required for the balance of steps.
6. Force the small end of the funnel into one end of the rubber tube.

34

7. Use the pencil to punch a small hole in the bottom of the cup. The hole should be just large enough for the other end of the rubber tube to slide through.
8. Secure the cup and tube with the masking tape.
9. Place the funnel over the chest and the cup over an ear and listen carefully to the sounds that our hearts make.

Can you answer the following questions from your observations?

1. On which side of your body is your heart, the left side or the right side?
2. What kind of noises does a heart make?
3. Could you hear it beat like a drum?
4. Did your classmates' or friends' hearts make the same sounds as your heart? If not, what was different about the sounds?

Teacher note. Now have the students jump up and down for a moment or two to get their hearts beating faster and repeat steps 8 and 9 in the instructions and repeat the questions.

Backyard Scientist solution to the experiment.

The sound of your heart beating was captured by the funnel and transmitted to your ear by the air inside the rubber/plastic tubing and paper cup. Doctors, nurses, and paramedics use stethoscopes to listen to people's hearts all the time. Veterinarians use stethoscopes to listen to our pets' hearts. Can you think of anyone else who might use a stethoscope?

Your heart is usually located in the left side of your chest. You should have been able to hear the thumping sound as it pumps the blood through your body. You may even have heard the swishing noise—the sound of your blood flowing through your heart valves, and your veins and arteries.

Most hearts are similar, but not exactly the same.

A doctor listening to your heart can tell if it is healthy or if there may be something that may need to be taken care of.

Teacher note. By holding the funnel at the students' upper back, they will be able to hear the air entering and leaving their lungs as they inhale and exhale.

This is a great project to use as a jumping off point to learning more about our bodies and other organs.

Experiment #18
The Iceberg Experiment

Do icebergs float?

Try the following Backyard Scientist experiment to discover the answer.

Gather the following supplies:
You will need access to a refrigerator with a freezer, 1 carton plain table salt, 2 identical size plastic mugs, 2 identical size large bowls, ruler, and enough cold water and hot water to fill bowls.

Start Experimenting.
Teacher assistance will be required.
1. Fill the two mugs with cold water from the tap and place in a freezer until frozen solid.
2. Fill one large bowl with hot water and dissolve as much salt in the water as you can and then let cool or place in refrigerator to speed this up.
3. Fill the other bowl with cold water from the tap.
4. Remove the frozen water from the two mugs (in one solid chunk) by running warm water over the outside until the ice comes free. An alternative is to let the mug sit in a bowl of warm water for a few minutes until the ice slides free.
5. Place one iceberg in each bowl of water.

6. Use the ruler to measure how far out of the water each iceberg will float.

Can you answer the following questions from your observations?

1. Did your icebergs float or sink to the bottom of the bowl?
2. Was part of your iceberg out of the water and part under the water?
3. Which iceberg floated higher in the water? The one in the water with the salt or the one in plain water?
4. Where do you think you might find real icebergs?
5. Where do they come from?
6. How big do you think they can be?
7. Can icebergs be dangerous to boats and ships?

Backyard Scientist solution to the experiment.

You made a model of an iceberg. Our model has a smooth surface, but real ones may have jagged and sharp edges. The "iceberg" we placed in the bowl of salt water (this is like the water in the oceans) did not sink as far into the water as did the iceberg that was in the bowl containing the "fresh" water (water without the salt). This is because the water with the salt is more **dense** and held the iceberg higher up.

Icebergs are found in the oceans. They are formed at the north and south poles of the earth where temperatures get very cold. Large chunks of ice break off (called calving) from ice shelves and glaciers and float to warmer climates on ocean currents. These large floating islands of ice can be bigger than your house and can be a danger to ships. A large iceberg can easily tear a hole in a big ship.

Because of the difference in density of icebergs which are made up of frozen fresh water and the salt water of the oceans, as much as 7/8 of the iceberg is below the surface of the ocean. This means we can only see the "tip" of the iceberg or a small portion of it sticking out of the water. A ship could be hundreds of yards from the part of the iceberg that can be seen, but still run into the part of the iceberg that is below the water and therefore cannot be seen.

It is also hard to predict or guess where icebergs will travel. Icebergs are pushed in the direction that the winds are blowing and ocean currents are flowing.

Teacher note. You may want to show a picture of an iceberg to the class.

Experiment #19
Fun with Surface Tension

Can you make water stand on a penny?

Try the following Backyard Scientist experiment to discover the answer.

Gather the following supplies:
One medicine dropper or a plastic straw to use as a pipette, 1 ounce of water, 1 two- to four ounce cup and a penny.

Start Experimenting.
1. Observe the penny carefully. Note its shape, size, color, temperature, design, etc.

Teacher note. All the experiments in this book promote **predicting**. Have your students predict how many drops of water will fit on a penny.

38

2. Use the dropper or straw to transfer water from the cup to the penny one drop at a time until no more water will stay on the penny.

Teacher note. It will take a little practice if you are using straws. Dip one end of the straw into the water. Then cover the other end with a finger or thumb. Next place the straw over the penny and release the finger so that one drop of water at a time falls onto the penny. You may want to have parents <u>wash</u> and save medicine droppers that come with various medicines.

Can you answer the following questions from your observations?

1. How many drops of water were you able to fit onto your penny?

Teacher note. Since some students may not be able to count the water drops let them use dry peas or other small objects as counting tools. Have them move one object to a pile for each drop of water and have them "count" their drops one at a time.

2. Was this number close to your prediction?
3. Did the little drops become one large drop of water?
4. What caused the bulging shape of the water bubble that formed on your penny?
5. Why didn't the water run or fall off your penny?

Backyard Scientist solution to the experiment.

The penny held a lot of water drops without any falling off. At some point, when there were just too many water **molecules,** the water fell off the penny. Scientists have a code for molecules. The code for water is H_2O. That means there are two **atoms** of **hydrogen** and one atom of **oxygen** in each molecule of water. Both hydrogen and oxygen are gases in the air we breathe.

Water molecules have a very strong attraction for each other—just like magnets attract one another. We call the attraction between water molecules **surface tension**. Scientists call surface tension **molecular cohesion**. The water molecules are tugging at one another with a strong and equal force in all directions, except at the very **surface**. There are no water molecules pulling upward on the very top.

Additional experimenting. Try this same experiment using other liquids like milk, liquid soap, rubbing alcohol, syrup or whatever you have on hand. You will obtain different results with these, except for the alcohol. Because the alcohol we buy is mostly water and alcohol has low molecular cohesion, most of the alcohol molecules will evaporate leaving behind only water which will yield the similar results as in the experiment above.

_____

_____

_____

Experiment #20
Molecular Cohesion

Do molecules attract and repel like magnets?

Try the following Backyard Scientist experiment to discover the answer.

Gather the following supplies:
1 piece of wax paper about 12 inches long, 1 eye dropper, a cup of water, toothpicks and food coloring (optional).

Start Experimenting.
1. Add some food coloring to the water if you wish.
2. Place the wax paper on the table (you may have to put something on the corners to prevent it from curling up—erasers work well).
3. Use the eye dropper to place about six to eight drops of water on the wax paper.
4. Wet the tips of the toothpicks.
5. Place the tip of the toothpick as close as you can over a drop of water on the wax paper but don't touch the drop of water with the toothpick.
6. Repeat, growing different size (small to large) drops of water on the wax paper.

Can you answer the following questions from your observations?

1. What shape were the drops of water that you placed on the wax paper?
2. Did the drops of water on the wax paper try to jump onto the wet end of the toothpicks?
3. How close did you have to get to get the water drops to jump toward the wet end of the toothpicks?
4. Did placing larger drops of water on the wax paper make any difference in how they were attracted to the toothpicks?
5. Why do you think this might have happened?

Backyard Scientist solution to the experiment.

The water drops on the wax paper looked like little balls of water. This is because water **molecules** have a strong **affinity** for each other. Scientists call this affinity, **molecular cohesion**—pretty big words.

You should also have seen that there was a strong attraction between the drops of water on the wax paper and the wet end of the toothpick. The drops of water on the wax paper tended to move to the wet end of the toothpick.

This affinity is a result of the water molecule having a positive (+) and a negative (−) electrical charge. Yes, **molecules** have electrical charges. Things with opposite charges attract one another. Things with the same charges **repel** each other. The size of the drop of water really did not have any effect on the experiment.

Teacher note. To further demonstrate the idea of opposite charges attracting and the same charge repelling, use some small magnets. Kids love these.

If you have a magnetic wand (available at many toy stores), try placing it over the water drops on the wax paper and compare these results with the original experiment results.

NOTES.

_____

_____

_____

Experiment #21
Exploring Plants

What do you think plants need in order to grow big and strong like you?

Try the following Backyard Scientist experiment to discover the answer.

Gather the following supplies:
2 empty and clean egg shell halves, potting soil (or substitute sifted dirt from the garden) to fill egg shells, egg cartons cut to hold two egg shells, assorted felt tip markers, a cup of water, 4 to 6 watercress seeds, a plastic spoon, and a calendar (optional).

Teacher note. You can also have the students make small egg cups from clay to support the egg shells during this experiment.

Start Experimenting.
1. Use the markers to draw faces on the egg shells. Handle them carefully so they don't break.
2. With the spoon, fill the shells with potting soil or sifted dirt from the garden.

3. Sprinkle two or three watercress seeds on top of the soil in each shell.
4. Gently press these into the soil.
5. Moisten the soil with a little water. Don't over water.
6. Place the egg shells in the egg cartons so they will not roll or tilt.
7. Water regularly as needed adding only a little water each time.
8. Place one egg shell in a lighted area of the room (near a window is great).
9. Place the other egg shell and its supporting egg carton in a closet, cupboard or box so light does not reach the seeds.
10. Observe your shells for a couple of weeks.

Can you answer the following questions from your observations?

1. What kind of plant will grow in your egg shell?
2. Will each seed turn into a plant?
3. Do you know what watercress is and for what it is used?
4. What are the things all plants need so they grow big, strong and healthy, much like you?
5. How would you compare the plant you grew in the lighted area with the plant you grew where it could not get any light?

Backyard Scientist solution to the experiment.

The seeds you planted and placed where they could get light grew into watercress plants. Young watercress plants look a little like the grass we like to play on. We use watercress in salads and on sandwiches.

All of the watercress seeds received water when you watered the soil. They also received the **nutrients** they needed (**calcium** and other **minerals)** from the egg shell. The seeds that were in the light, quickly **germinated** and **sprouted** "hairs" that stood straight up out of the soil. The seeds that were placed in the dark may not have grown at all, or if they did, the plants did not look healthy.

Most seeds grow quickly when they get everything they need. To grow into healthy and strong plants, seeds need: water, food, and light. People and animals that live on the land need the same things to be strong and healthy. Most fish, but not all need the same to grow. Some fish live so deep in the ocean that no sun light gets there. These have adapted to their lightless environment

Teacher note. It might be fun to time the various stages of growth, first time you can see the plant emerge from the soil, time to first leaf, etc. Use and mark a calendar for this. You may want to repeat the experiment using parsley seeds, grass seeds, etc.

Experiment #22
Is it Really Empty?

Does air take up space?

Try the following Backyard Scientist experiment to discover the answer.

CLEAR PLASTIC CUP

Gather the following supplies:
1 deep bowl or large jar, 1 pan large enough to accommodate the bowl and catch any water that may flow out of it, 1 clear six to eight ounce plastic cup, enough water to fill the bowl to the rim.

Start Experimenting.
1. Slowly add the water to the bowl until it is filled to the rim.

2. Push the cup, mouth down, slowly into the bowl.
3. Carefully observe the cup and the water.

Can you answer the following questions from your observations?

1. Did the water enter the cup when you pushed it down into the water?
2. Did you see any bubbles leave the cup?
3. Can you think of some machines that operate on or use compressed air?

Backyard Scientist solution to the experiment.

You observed that the water entered a little way into the plastic cup. No air bubbles should have come out of the plastic cup. The air that was in the cup before we placed the cup in the water was forced into a smaller space by the water entering the cup. Because there was air in the cup, water could not fill up all of the space in the cup. The air filled the space that the water did not fill. From this experiment, we can see that air does take up space. The space in the room we are in that is not taken up by the students, teacher and furniture is taken up by air.

Water, air and other things are made up of **atoms** and **molecules**. When the molecules of air are forced closer together, we say that they are **compressed**. When compressed air is released, it can power machines.

A lot of machines operate using compressed air. Here are some things that I thought of: the tool dentists sometimes use to clean your teeth, machines that mechanics use to loosen and tighten the wheels on cars.

When you blow air into a balloon, you are compressing the air inside. When you let go of the balloon, the air escapes and the balloon flies around in crazy ways. That is because the compressed air is not **controlled** in any way.

NOTES.

_____

_____

_____

_____

Experiment #23
The Human-size Bubble

Can you put a person into a bubble?

Try the following Backyard Scientist experiment to discover the answer.

HOSE CLAMP

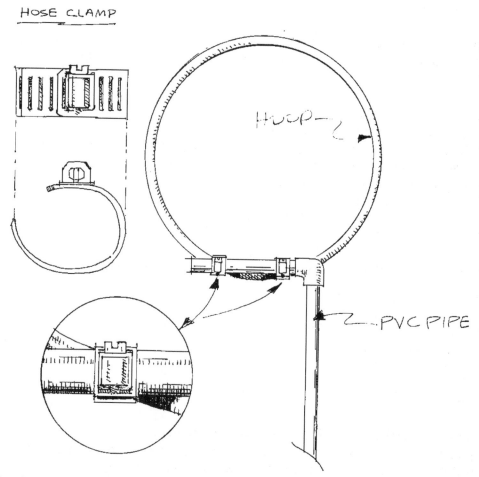

HOOP—?

—PVC PIPE

Gather the following supplies:
For wand: 1 hula hoop, 5 ft. of ¾" diameter PVC pipe (thin wall), 1 ea. ¾" T-connector, 1 ea. ¾" 90 degree couple, 2 ea. Size 12 (1-1/4" size) hose clamps, hacksaw, screw driver, ruler, rigid plastic wading pool (inflatable vinyl will not work), and a milk crate or small plastic step. For **bubble solution:** 46 ounces Joy or Dawn concentrated dishwashing detergent or 69 ounces of not concentrated, 10 gallons bottled or filtered water, 16 ounces liquid glycerin. Safety goggles or eye glasses when getting into the bubble..

Teacher note. Assemble the bubble wand in advance. Cut one piece of the PVC pipe 8" long. Cut the T-connector so that it will clamp over the hula hoop with the hose connectors. Using the screw driver, tighten the hose connectors over the

46

hula hoop and the two pieces of the T-connector. Insert the 8" long piece of PVC pipe into the remaining hole of the connector, then place the 90 degree elbow over the other end of the 8" length of PVC pipe. Connect the remaining piece of PVC pipe to the other opening in the *elbow*. You can use PVC cement if you want to make connections permanent. **This sounds complicated, but it is not. Just do one step at a time.**

Make up the bubble solution a few days ahead of time. Adjust as needed by adding more soap or glycerin. When finished, store in gallon or larger containers to do again.

Start Experimenting.
1. Let the students observe and help make the bubble solution.
2. When ready, place the plastic milk crate in the center of the plastic pool.
3. Have a student stand on the milk crate with hands at their side.
4. Place the wand over the student's head and into the solution.
5. When the wand is thoroughly wetted, slowly raise the wand over the student's head—note static electricity on dry days can make the bubble stick to clothes and pop.

Can you answer the following questions from your observations?
1. What did things look like from inside the bubble?
2. Did they look different than if you were not in a bubble?
3. Did you see the bubble make different shapes?
4. Did you see different colors in the bubble?
5. What caused the bubble to finally pop?
6. Did the bubble try to stick to you or your clothes?

Backyard Scientist solution to the experiment.
The soap and water molecules stick to each other in a strong bond and make the bubble flexible so it can easily change shape without breaking. The glycerin molecules are used to keep the bubble from drying too quickly. The reason bubbles break is that they get a dry spot and the bond between molecules breaks.

Bubbles have an electric charge. If you or your clothes have a lot of static electricity on them, the bubble is attracted to you just like magnets attract things that contain iron.

The different colors you saw on the bubble were caused by the light being bent into their different wave lengths. We call this bending **refraction**. It is the same reason we sometimes see rainbows after it rains.

Things looked different when you were inside the bubble because of the bending of the light as it entered the bubble.

Experiment #24
Potential and Kinetic Energy

Can you make a coffee can automatically return to you using two forms of energy?

Try the following Backyard Scientist experiment to discover the answer.

Gather the following supplies:

1 metal coffee can (empty), 1 plastic cover from the coffee can, 1 strong rubber band, some weights (lead sinkers, washers or a small piece of iron pipe), 2 wooden kitchen matches, a nail, a hammer, a file, a ruler, and a pencil or marker.

Start Experimenting.

1. Using the ruler, find the center of the coffee can bottom and mark it with the pencil or marker.
2. Do the same to the plastic lid.

Teacher note and advance preparation. It is important that both holes are as close to the center as is possible.

3. Punch a hole in the center of the coffee can bottom.
4. Punch a hole in the center of the plastic lid.
5. File the holes smooth so they don't cut the rubber band.
6. Thread the rubber band through the hole in the bottom of the can.
7. Keep the rubber band from slipping out by inserting a match stick through the loop in the rubber band.

8. Securely attach the weights to the rubber band—about midway between the top and bottom of the can.
9. Pull the remaining end of the rubber band through the hole in the plastic lid and insert the other match stick in the loop so the rubber band does not slip out.
10. Slip the plastic lid securely over the open end of the coffee can.
11. Roll it on the floor or outside on the driveway.
12. Just before it stops, order the can to return to you.

Can you answer the following questions from your observations?

1. Did the coffee can roll slower toward the end of the roll than in the beginning?
2. What made the coffee can return to you?

Backyard Scientist solution to the experiment.

In this experiment, we studied two forms of energy. One kind of energy is called **potential energy**. The other form of energy we studied was **kinetic energy**. Potential energy is energy that is stored in an object. Kinetic energy is energy in a moving object.

In this experiment, the initial rolling of the can caused the winding of the rubber band by the weights that you attached to it. As the can rolled, the rubber band began to twist. The more the rubber band twisted, the more potential energy was stored in it. So, if your can rolled a long way, you were able to store a lot of potential energy.

When released, the rubber band unwound converting the potential energy into kinetic energy. Once the rubber band gave up all of its potential energy, the kinetic energy of the moving can began to twist the rubber band in the opposite direction. This potential energy was then converted into kinetic energy resulting in the can returning to you.

The rolling action of the can demonstrated kinetic energy—the energy of a moving object. It takes energy to stop something from moving. The laws of physics tell us that objects in motion want to stay in motion and those at rest want to stay at rest (stationary).

Can you think of other forms of potential energy? How about water behind a dam? The stored water is potential energy until it flows through large pipes to turn turbines attached to electric generators.

Can you think of another example of kinetic energy? How about your parents' car as it moves down the street? It wants to stay in motion forever. However, it will slow because of several factors such as air resistance and friction of parts of the car and the tires on the pavement. Your parents apply energy (friction) in the form of brakes to overcome the kinetic energy of the car when they want to stop at a signal.

Experiment #25
Molecular Diffusion

Do molecules stick together?

Try the following Backyard Scientist experiment to discover the answer.

Gather the following supplies:
1 tsp. vanilla extract, 1 balloon, a small funnel, and a watch, clock or timer.

Start Experimenting.
1.   Insert the funnel into the neck of the balloon.

2. Carefully pour the vanilla extract into the balloon. Try not to get any on the outside surfaces of the balloon.
3. Inflate the balloon and quickly tie it so that no air escapes from the neck of the balloon.
4. Shake the balloon for about 30 seconds. Use the clock or other timing device to keep track of the time.
5. Now smell the outside of the balloon.

Can you answer the following questions from your observations?

1. Were you able to smell the vanilla from outside the balloon?
2. Can you describe the smell of vanilla?
3. How do you think it was possible to smell the vanilla since we poured the vanilla inside the balloon, did not spill any on the outside and then tied the balloon closed?

Teacher note. You might want to make a chart and record the reasons that the students give.

Backyard Scientist solution to the experiment.

You could easily smell the sweet smell of the vanilla extract outside the balloon. Vanilla extract contains alcohol. Alcohol molecules have very low **molecular cohesion**. That means they do not stick together for long and they evaporate into the air.

In vanilla extract, some of the vanilla molecules attach themselves to the alcohol molecules. There are very small spaces between the **latex** molecules that make the balloon. The spaces are so small that we cannot see them without a good **microscope**.

A microscope is used by scientists to see very small things. It is a little like a very powerful magnifying glass.

The vanilla extract molecules that were attached to the alcohol molecules escaped from the inside of the balloon by sneaking through the spaces between the latex molecules. Scientist call this **diffusion**.

Scientists use diffusion for many purposes. A use for molecular diffusion is to make fresh drinking water from salty ocean water. This process is used where there is very little rain fall and a lot of people that need drinking water, like in Saudi Arabia.

Experiment #26
Discovering Isopods

Do you have the fastest isopod?

Try the following Backyard Scientist experiment to discover the answer.

Gather the following supplies:

A friend or two, a few plastic cups or plastic zip close bags, magnifying lens, 8-1/2" x 11" piece of paper, tape, yard stick, chalk and a small shovel or large spoon for digging.

Teacher note. Before your students can begin this experiment, they will have to know what isopods look like. Isopods are **crustaceans** that have flat, **oval** bodies, short **abdomens**, and, usually seven pairs of similar legs. They are grey or black in color. Often they are referred to as pill bugs, potato bugs, or roly-poly bugs.

Start Experimenting.

Part One *with teacher supervision and assistance*.

1. Punch a few small holes in the zip close bags so your specimens can breathe.
2. Take a digging tool and with a partner, go on an expedition to find some isopods. *Where? Try a grassy area with flower beds, gardens, parks or vacant lots. Isopods like to hang out in dark, moist, undisturbed spots where there is lots of* **decaying** *plant material. Look under boards, logs, rocks, piles of leaves or grass cuttings.* **Don't pick up any other kind of creature like spiders or scorpions.**

3. Gently pick up the isopods and place them in your collecting cup or collecting bag. *Remember, isopods are living creatures and we must respect them and handle them carefully.*
4. Add some of the soil and decaying plant material from where you found your isopods.
5. Use your magnifying lens to carefully examine each isopod that you collected. Look at its head, body, tail, legs, and color.
6. Observe what the isopods are doing in their container.

Part Two.
7. Now it's time for our isopod race. Use the yard stick and chalk to draw a circle 18 to 24 inches in diameter.
8. Roll the paper into cones and tape to hold closed.
9. Cut off the tip of the cones to make about a half inch opening.
10. Place the narrow end of your funnel in the center of the circle.
11. Select your "best or favorite" isopod and gently place it into the wide end of the cone.
12. On the count of three, everyone lifts their cone to gently slide out their isopod.
13. The first isopod to cross the chalk line is the winner of our isopod race.
14. After we have completed studying the isopods and the race is finished, let's release the isopods back where we found them.

Can you answer the following questions from your observations?

1. Were all the isopods that you collected the same color?
2. Were they all about the same size?
3. Were you able to see the head, abdomen and tail?
4. How many pairs of legs did your isopods have?
5. What were the isopods doing when they were in your collection cups or bags?
6. What did they eat?
7. Were there any common characteristics about the isopods that came in first, second or third in our race?

Backyard Scientist solution to the experiment.

Isopods are **crustaceans** that have flat, oval bodies, short **abdomens**, and, usually have seven pairs of similar legs. They are grey or black in color. Often they are referred to as pill bugs, potato bugs, or roly-poly bugs. Some are larger than others, but when you find them in groups, they are usually of the same size. When isopods sense danger, they may roll up into a ball and stay that way until they think the danger has passed. Did your isopods roll up into a ball?

You should have counted 14 legs on your isopods. Fourteen legs is just like saying seven pairs of legs. You wear two shoes or one pair of shoes. A pair is the same as saying two of something.

Glossary of Terms

abdomen n. the hind portion of the body behind the thorax in an anthropoid

absolute pitch n. Music. The ability to identify any pitch heard or produce any pitch referred to by name (do, re, me, fa, so la, te, do)

absorb v. 1: to suck up or take up <a sponge *absorbs* water> <plant roots *absorb* water> **2:** top receive without echo <provide with a sound-*absorbing* surface>

affinity n. an attractive force between substances or particles that causes them to enter into and remain in chemical combination

atom n. 1: the smallest particle of an element that can exist either alone or in combination **2:** the atom considered as a source of vast energy

buoyancy n. 1: the tendency of a body to float or rise when in a fluid <the buoyancy of a cork in water> **2:** the power of a fluid to put an upward force on a body placed in it <the buoyancy of seawater>

burrow v. 1: to construct by tunneling **2:** to hide oneself in or as if in a burrow

calcium n. a silver-white metallic element that is found only in combination (as in limestone) and is one of the necessary elements making up the bodies of most plants and animals

capillaries n. capillary tubes; *especially* : any of the tiny hairlike blood vessels connecting arteries and veins

carbon dioxide n. a heavy, colorless gas that does not support burning, dissolves in water to form carbonic acid, is formed especially by the burning and breaking down of organic substances (as in animal respiration<breathing>, is absorbed from the air by plants in photosynthesis, and has many industrial uses

cells n. one of the tiny units that are basic building blocks of living things, that carry on the basic functions of life either alone or in groups, and that include a nucleus and are surrounded by a membrane

CO_2 n. see carbon dioxide

Cohesion n. molecular attraction by which particles of a body are united throughout the mass

compressed v. 1: to press or become pressed together **2:** having a high mass per unit of volume <carbon dioxide is a *dense* gas>

controlled v. to keep within limits

crustaceans n. any of a large class of mostly water-dwelling arthropods such as lobsters, shrimps, crabs, wood lice, water flees, and barnacles; all having an exoskeleton

dense adj. 1: marked by compactness or crowding together of parts **2:** having a high mass per unit of volume <carbon dioxide is a *dense* gas>

diffusion n. the mixing of particles of liquids, gases, or solids so that they move from a region of concentration to one of lower concentration

displaced v. removed physically out of position <water *displaced* by a floating object>

dissolved v. to mix or cause to mix with a liquid so that the result is a liquid that is the same throughout <salt *dissolves* in water>

electric adj. relating to, or operated by electricity

energy n. 1: the capacity for doing work **2:** usable poser (as heat, light, or electricity) **synonym:** POWER

environmentalist n. one concerned about <u>environmental</u> quality especially of the <u>environment</u> with respect to the control of pollution

evaporated v. 1: to have passed off or cause to pass of into vapor from a liquid state **2:** to have removed some of the water from (as by heating)

force n. an influence (as a push or pull) that tends to produce a change in the speed or direction of motion of something <the *force* of gravity>

friction n. 1: the rubbing of one body against another **2:** the force that resists relative motion between two bodies in contact

germinated v. 1: to have caused to sprout or develop **2:** to have begun to grow **: SPROUT**

gravity n. the <u>gravitational</u> attraction of the mass of the earth, the moon, or a planet for bodies at or near its surface **2:** a fundamental physical force that is responsible for interactions between matter (as stars and planets), and between particles (as photons) and aggregations of matter—called also *gravitation, gravitational force*

H_2O n. chemical symbol for water representing two atoms of hydrogen and one atom of oxygen

high-pitched adj. high in pitch, as a voice or musical tone

hydrogen n. a chemical element that is the simplest and lightest of all chemical elements and is normally found alone as a colorless, odorless, highly flammable gas having two atoms per molecule

inertia n. a property of matter by which it remains at rest or in unchanging motion unless acted on by some external force

interpret v. to explain the meaning of <*interpret* the vibrations> <to *interpret* the teacher's instructions>

kazoo n. an instrument that imparts a buzzing quality to the human voice and that usually consists of a small metal or plastic tuve with a side hole covered by a thin membrane

kinetic energy n. energy associated with motion

latex n. a milky juice produced by the cells of various plants (as milkweeds, poppies, and the rubber tree)

light n. 1: something that makes vision possible **2:** the sensation aroused by stimulation of the visual receptors **3:** an electromagnetic radiation in the wavelength range including infrared, visible, ultraviolet, and X rays and traveling in a vacuum with a speed of about 186,281 miles (300,000 kilometers) per second; **specifically :** the part of this range that is visible to the human eye

low-pitched adj. low in pitch, as a voice or musical tone

microscope n. an optical instrument consisting of a lens or a combination of lenses for making enlarged or magnified images or minute objects

minerals n. 1: a solid chemical element or compound (as diamond or quartz) that occurs naturally in the form of crystals and results from process not involving living or once-living matter **2:** a naturally occurring substance (as ore, or petroleum) obtained usually from the ground

molecule n. the smallest particle of a substance that retains all the properties of the substance and is composed of one or more atoms

motion n. an act, process, or instance of changing place **: MOVEMENT**

nerve impulse n. an electric charge that moves along a nerve fiber after it is stimulated and that carries a record of sensation or an instruction to act

nuclear energy n. energy that can be set free by changes in the nucleus of an atom (as by fission or a heavy nucleus or fusion of a light nuclei into heavier ones with accompanying loss of mass)

nutrients n. nutrient substances or ingredients (substances that are used as a food)

optical illusion n. a misleading image presented to the eye

ornithologist n. a person who studies ornithology, a branch of zoology dealing with birds

oxygen n. an element that is found free as a colorless, tasteless, odorless gas, forms about 21 percent of the atmosphere, is capable of combining with almost all elements, and is necessary for life

P$_h$ n. a number used in expressing acidity or alkalinity on a scale whose values run from 0 to 14 with 7 representing neutrality, numbers less than 7 increasing acidity, and numbers greater than 7 increasing alkalinity

polymer n. a chemical compound or mixture of compounds that is formed by a combination of smaller molecules and consists basically or repeating structural units

potential energy n. the amount of energy a thing (as a weight raised to a height or a coiled spring) has because of its position or because the arrangement of its parts

pressure n. 1: the action of a force against an opposing force **2:** the force applied over a surface divided by its area

repel v. to force away or apart or tend to do so by mutual action at a distance <two like electrical charges *repel* each other>

resistance n. an opposing or slowing force

sound wave n. a wave formed by compression of the material (as air) though which it travels regardless of whether it can be heard

support v. to hold up or serve as a foundation or prop for <buildings>

surface n. the outside of an object or body

surface tension n. the attractive force exerted upon the surface molecules of a liquid by the molecules beneath that tends to draw the surface molecules into the bulk of the liquid and makes the liquid assume the shape having the least surface area

structural adj. used in building structures

vibrate v. to move or cause to move back and forth or from side to side

Notes